FORGED PRESCRIPIONS

TONY O'NEILL

STORIES:

FORGED PRESCRIPTIONS is dedicated to Vanessa and Nico O'Neill, without whom there would be no books, no love, and no reason.

1
EXQUISITE CORPSE

"My name is Joe, and I am an addict."

Hi Joe.

They were in a small church basement somewhere in East Hollywood. The Wednesday morning "Happy Hour" Narcotics Anonymous meeting was in full swing. Joe spoke hesitatingly to the small group of ex-junkies, drunks, tweakers, and crackheads, looking like the sickest person in the room. A defeated-looking heroin addict in his late 40s, Joe's face was patterned with deep creases, and his eyes trembled in their sockets like furtive crackheads in a by-the-hour motel room. Underneath the crumpled long-sleeve shirt, both his arms were crisscrossed with decades of needle tracks.

Sitting with her chair pushed up against the back wall, next to a display of pamphlets with titles like *Too Young To Be An Alcoholic?* and *Can Atheists Join the Fellowship?* was Tania. An attractive woman in her early 30s, Tania absently chewed a hangnail as she watched Joe address the group. This was the second time she'd noticed this man at one of her regular meetings. Last week, she clocked him standing by the coffee urn at the Alcoholics Anonymous meeting at Hollywood and Highland, looking like a freshly interred corpse as he furtively filled his pockets with stale cookies. Now, he sat a few rows ahead of her, addressing the group in a barely audible monotone. He looked even worse than he had last week, she mused.

Tania glanced around the room. She guessed she was the only person under 40 here, although, she conceded, it's sometimes hard to tell with dope fiends. This meeting attracted the old timers, aging junkies with years of sobriety under their belt who circled the newcomers like sharks attracted to the scent of chum. She silently dubbed these kinds of meetings as *Elephant's Graveyards.* Tania had surprised even herself by coming here. She had already decided that this whole 12-step thing wasn't for her, after all. She'd woke up this morning with the unshakable certainty that this would be the day she gave in to her overwhelming urge to score dope. Before hitting her old scoring spots, she convinced herself to come to this final meeting. One last hour of her life, she reasoned, just to be sure. She's heard some in the program talk about "white light" experiences, a kind of spiritual bolt-from-the-blue that supposedly struck some addicts like lightning, utterly obliterating their obsession to use. She doubted the veracity of these reports but figured she had little to lose in giving God or the Universe or whatever the fuck was running this shit show one final chance to show her that it cared. That it even knew Tania existed. One last chance, then she could return to the dealers that haunted Macarthur Park, having given this sobriety thing the old college try.

"Well, uh..." Joe said, "I'm not feeling so hot today. I relapsed again... a little while ago, you know? It really fucking... took it out of me. I mean, physically, it took it *out* of me. Mentally, too, I guess... The thing is, I'm finding it hard even to get the... *focus*, you know, the focus to begin this whole process again... Working on my recovery, y'know? I... I'm a heroin addict, as I'm sure some of you know." He gave a forced, self-effacing smile that didn't suit his face. Some of the old-timers shot Joe encouraging smiles, urging him on. "I had a hundred and seventy-nine days under my belt, the best I've managed in a long time... But after I fell off? It's been rough. I honestly feel like I'm gonna struggle to make it to the end of the day without using. I wasn't even planning on coming to this meeting. I came in a kind of *trance*. I dunno what else to do."

Tania wiped her nose with the back of her hand. Fuck, shit, piss. The meeting was a mistake. What did she think would happen? It's not as if her disillusionment with sobriety was a recent development. She'd been clean -and miserable as hell about it - for a good seven months now. The miracle they promised her never arrived. After the painful detox, expensive inpatient treatment, and her stint in that crummy sober living house, nothing was *better*. Everything was still shit. She resented these meetings and especially hated the way the AA crowd spoke in a mixture of California-Zen spiritual homilies and sobriety catchphrases: *It works if you work it... Let go and let God...* What a fucking joke.

As rough as things could get when she was strung out, Tania mused, at least her habit gave her a reason to get out of bed in the morning. Without the relentless hustle for money and drugs to occupy Tania's waking hours, the days now seemed endless. When someone like Joe came in, fresh from a relapse, she didn't feel *bad* for them. She secretly wished she had been getting high *with* them, and their weak-ass apologies to the group just irritated her further.

The sober living home in Los Feliz had been a joke. She came there straight from a charity ward detox. She was 36 years old, for Chrissakes, far too old to be roommates with a meth-addled teenage moron from Orange County with perky tits and bad teeth. Her roomie talked so much that Tania could barely imagine what the bitch must have been like when she was tweaking. *Fuck this scene*, she'd told herself, hurriedly packing her bags, *I'm too old for this shit. Too smart. Something will come along, it always does.*

"...But I'm thankful to be here," Joe said, sounding anything but. "And I'm going to keep trying... Thanks."

"*Thanks, Joe.*"

When it was all over, they stood and held hands to recite the serenity prayer. *God, grant me the serenity to accept the things I cannot change...* In the years since her first meeting, Tania's reflexive indignation over the religious trappings of the program hadn't faded. She didn't believe in God any more than she believed in redemption. Tania knew that faith, prayer, and redemption were ridiculous concepts of use only to the most gullible morons imaginable. Plenty of people had told her not to get hung up on "the God stuff" or to '*fake it till you make it.*' That was another of those irritating mantras that were standard currency in these rooms. But *faking it* was never Tania's style. It seemed there would be no white light experience for her either; as the meeting ended, her mind was firmly made up. She was going to get high.

Everybody yelled: "*Keep coming back!*"

And just like that, the meeting was over.

Some folks began to leave, but a large portion of the members lingered behind, breaking into smaller groups to drink coffee, talk and bullshit. Tania scanned the room, catching a glimpse of Joe as he weaved through the crowd and made for the exit before anyone could intercept him. She hesitated for a moment before following.

He was halfway down the block by the time Tania made it outside.

"Joe? Hey, *Joe*!"

He hustled away from the meeting like a nervous shoplifter. She called him again; he picked up his pace in response. She sped up, closing the gap steadily until she was finally within reach of him.

"Hey, Joe!"

He finally stopped and looked her up and down, eyes radiating suspicion and irritation.

"It's just like the song," she said, giving him her best facsimile of an apologetic smile. Joe's face clouded over. "Song?"

"*Hey Joe.... Where you going with that gun in your hand?*" Tania sang, sweeping the hair out of her face. "I'm Tania, by the way."

"Oh, yeah... *that* song," Joe muttered. "Joe."

Joe's eyes darted between the corner and her expectant face as if planning an escape.

"Yeah, I know. I heard you speak. In the meeting."

Joe nodded slowly, unused to making small talk.

Tania removed her sunglasses, exposing eyes so dazzlingly green they momentarily caught Joe off guard.

"I was just wondering, d'you wanna go somewhere?" she asked. "Together, I mean?"

At this suggestion, Joe began backing away from her, babbling apologetically.

"Thing is... no time, y'know.... appointments. I'm actually on my way to see someone. If you wanted to grab a coffee... maybe another time?"

Tania suddenly understood his reluctance. *Coffee.*

Another in a long fucking line of AA clichés. When someone admits to wavering in their commitment, on the verge of a relapse or a crisis of faith, then a throng of do-gooders would spring into action. This impromptu intervention-cum-pep talk was usually framed as "going for coffee." Tania had been through this routine plenty herself, always suspecting it was more for the others' benefit than hers.

"I don't *want* to get coffee," she said. "It's nothing like that. Honestly... I just figured you might be able to help me. Who're you meeting?"

Joe seemed totally thrown off by this unexpected turn. Despite her taste for narcotics and the ugly lifestyle it had forced her into, Tania was undoubtedly an attractive woman. Six months off the needle had given her a veneer of health. There was color in her cheeks; her breasts were filling out again as she put on a little sobriety weight. She wore a long-sleeved Marc Bolan shirt despite the heat. Her hair was dyed blonde, her natural brunette growing out at the roots. Joe had not talked to a woman as attractive as Tania in what seemed like a lifetime. Like some tongue-tied teenage boy, he danced anxiously from foot to foot as he stammered out an answer.

"No one really, just meeting this guy... an old friend of mine."

Tania smiled like a cat. "Could this friend of yours maybe *get* something for me?"

Joe's eyes narrowed in suspicion. "What kind of something?"

"Come on. You know what I'm talking about, Joe."

Joe eyed her for any signs of duplicitousness but found none. "Maybe," he said finally. "Well... yeah, he can."

"Then could I, like, tag along? I've been out of the loop for a while, so you'd be helping me out big time."

"Ah. I mean... *maybe*...But, uh..."

"Spit it out, Joe," Tania said. "I'm a big girl. What's the problem?"

"It's just... Shit, Tania - I'm *broke*, okay? I've barely got enough bread to get myself straightened out."

Tania shook her head at this. "Shit! I'm not looking for a freebie or nuthin'. I pay my own way... I just need a hook-up, is all. Cleaned-up a while back and deleted all my old contacts... you know how that goes. You kinda said you were back on, so I figured you could make the introduction, is all. Maybe we can hang out later... if that's cool?"

"Sure," Joe said. "I guess that's cool with me..."

Tania grinned as she hooked her arm around his.

"Lead the way, Joe..." she said. "Times a wasting!"

They headed downtown in Joe's battered Honda. As he drove, Joe explained that this guy operated out of a loft space near Pershing Square.

"His shit is always good quality, his measures are fair. He's choosy about who he sells to, that's why he's been in business for so long. I've been buying from him for almost two years," Joe said.

Tania nodded. "He delivers?"

"Nope," Joe said, shaking his head. "He doesn't do credit, either... gets pissy if you ask. There's a system... We gotta page ahead when we're around the corner. He's got this whole code worked out."

Tania's brow furrowed. "What kinda code?"

"He has dope, powder coke, and rock, see? They each have a code number. So you page the amount first, then what you want. Like, 201 would be a 20-bag of dope. 202 a twenty-dollar bindle of powder coke, 203 a twenty-dollar rock. A bundle of dope is 300, an 8-ball of coke is 400. Think that's it. It sounds complicated, but it's pretty easy. I'm usually in and out quick, no fucking around."

"Cool..." Tania said, nodding slowly. The whole system sounded ludicrous, but it didn't matter. She was going to get high, and that's all that mattered.

After finding an empty meter, Joe led Tania to the graffiti-scarred payphone he always used. Dropped a quarter in the slot, waited for the beeps, and put the order through. True to her word, Tania had cash, so they pooled their money and ordered a bundle of heroin and 40 dollars of crack. After he hung up, Tania imagined she could taste the sweet ammonia tang of the rock cocaine already, and her heart began to hammer in anticipation.

Joe brought her to a featureless steel door sandwiched between a grimy-looking fried chicken joint and ramshackle *botanica* called *Los Eternitad*. He rang the buzzer three times, and a voice crackled from the intercom. *Yeah?*

"It's Joe, I just beeped."

Whossat with jou?

"Friend of mine. She's cool."

This was followed by a silence that made Tania's breath catch in her throat. Then with a loud buzz, the door clicked open.

They stepped inside a dimly cool corridor, leading to an elevator with an out-of-order sign taped across it. They began to trudge up the stairs. The damp concrete stairwell reeked of piss and bleach. As they approached the fourth floor, Tania saw there were a couple of young punk girls waiting up ahead. Joe and Tania took their place in line. The punks were decked out in matching battered leather jackets and motorcycle boots and spoke to each other in whispers, sweating through their thick make-up.

"Man," Joe said. "They're busy today..."

Joe leaned against the wall and closed his eyes, with the resigned demeanor of a man well used to waiting around in dank stairways. From downstairs Tania heard someone being buzzed in, followed by the sound of approaching footsteps. She glanced down to see a scrawny white kid, in a Lakers shirt and baggy jeans, scurrying toward them. He was young, she guessed mid-twenties, with a pinched, rodent face and short-cropped peroxide-blonde hair. He got in line behind Joe and Tania, panting loudly. Tania avoided looking at him, but it was obvious the newcomer was looking at her, eager to speak. Finally, he gave Tania a gentle nudge.

"Yo... you with him?" he asked, nodding to Joe.

"That's right."

"Cool, man... Very cool..." he said, in a thick Russian accent. "How long you wait?"

Joe opened one lizard-like eye to look the kid over, before closing it again and continuing to ignore him. Tania sighed and said, "Not long."

That seemed to satisfy him for a few moments, but soon enough he began coughing. It was okay, at first, but grew gradually more theatrical. Getting no response, he nudged Tania again.

"Sorry for coughing," he said. "I'm very *sick*, today. Not good."

Tania tried to ignore him, but his spastic energy was putting her nerves on edge.

"Yo, check this out..." he continued, warming to his point. "I was right here, this morning -no? I been coming to this guy *forever*. This morning... I buy from him, yeah? I didn't feel *shit*, man. Seems his stuff is getting worse, no?"

Tania ignored him, focusing on the door at the top of the stairs willing for the line to move. Realizing she was ignoring him, the man began muttering darkly in Russian. Joe caught her eye, giving his head a little shake as if to say, *Don't talk to crazies.*

Finally, the door at the top of the stairs opened and small, skinny Latin kid, no more than 12 or 13 years old, emerged. From behind him, an anxious-looking man in a cheap suit, forehead slick with sweat, hurried out. He bounded down the stairs two at a time, disappearing out of sight as the stairs as the kid looked at the line, counting silently. Then he nodded at the girls, who handed over the money before the three of them headed back inside.

Joe and Tania took a few steps forward, their place at the head of the line. Tania felt her guts churning in familiar anticipation. The first hit after a while off is always glorious, like coming back to your childhood home and finding it exactly as you'd remembered it in your most rose-tinted recollections. Standing in this piss-stinking concrete stairwell, she felt Joe looked more solid... healthier, somehow. He seemed more *real* than before. It was as if, in his natural element, he had taken on an extra dimension. That craggy face could almost be taken for handsome, in a damaged kind of way. A minute or two dragged by. Finally, the kid returned followed by the punks, who scurried past Tania, giggling excitedly. Joe handed the bills to the kid, as he took them inside.

"'sup Joe?" the kid said, after counting the bills. "Who's your friend?"

"This is Tania, she's an old friend. She's cool."

"Bueno," the kid said. Then he touched his chest and said, "Paco. Is pleasure, si?"

"Nice to meet you, Paco..."

As they approached the large, steel door Joe asked, "How's the stuff today? All good?"

At this, the kid stopped short, looking puzzled.

"Whatchoo mean, *all good*? Is *always* good, jou know that, man..."

"I just mean... Is it the same stuff as yesterday?"

"Yeah, man..." Paco said, exasperated. "Is the same stuff as yesterday... Why jou askit this?"

"The guy out there was going on and on about how the *chiva* from this morning was bunk," Joe said, with an apologetic shrug. "Like, *muy malo*. Said he copped this morning and didn't even feel it."

Paco was visibly agitated now. He muttered something in Spanish, before pointing back to the stairs.

"This motherfucker?" Paco said. "This motherfucker... is *crazy*. Mess up in the head. Always askit for credit. Get mad when we say to... fuck off, jou know? He's make it the *trouble*. Maybe after today... no more. Eight-six, jou know?"

"I get it," Joe said. "Just figured I'd check, no offense..."

"Jou *know* us, homie. Is *all* good, man."

"Bueno," Joe said as Paco typed a code into the keypad, then pushed the door open.

They stepped inside. The room beyond was a huge, desolate loft space, with three men inside. The only furnishings were a TV with an X-box attached, a leather couch, and a coffee table. The windows were blocked out with black sheets. A bald man-mountain in a wife-beater sat in front of the TV, engrossed in a game of *Grand Theft Auto*. A gun was casually poking out of the waistband of his shorts. On the couch were two men, dressed in chinos and button-down shirts. One was shaved bald, with a wispy mustache. The other had long, straggly hair and a goatee. On the table was a shoebox full of money, two handguns, a weighing scale, and a book. Tania smiled to herself when she was what it was: *How to Get Rich* by Donald Trump. From a boombox in a corner of the room came the voice of Juan Gabriel, delivering a dramatic love ballad. The guy with the goatee was counting bills into stacks of a hundred, before bundling them with rubber bands. He did it with such practiced efficiency that Tania couldn't help staring at his hands.

Paco handed the money to the mustache, which was added to the pile. His partner handed over the shit. When Paco gave it to Joe, she noticed it was all sorted into a series of neat, color-coded ballons. Joe popped them into his mouth, using his tongue to maneuver them into the space between his gums and lip in case of a bust.

"See you around, man..." the mustache said.

"Gracias," Joe replied. "This is my friend, Tania. She's good people, I can vouch for her."

The mustache nodded. "Ola, Tania. Maybe I see you again."

"Count on it," Tania said, smiling.

"Let's go..."

Paco was already standing by the door, waiting for Joe and Tania. As they approached, Paco pulled back the latch and wrenched the door open. As he did this, there was a sudden rush of activity. In the confusion, Tania momentarily thought it was a bust. *Just my fucking luck,* she thought. *This dude's been operating for years and the moment I get an introduction, the fucking pigs close him down.* But then she realized it wasn't the police who'd come rushing into the room, unannounced. It was the Russian and he was waving a handgun around, with the snot still streaming from his nose. Paco yelled in surprise and indignation as the Russian grabbed him by the shirt and put the gun to his temple.

"Be cool," the Russian said. "Nobody fucking move!"

There were yells and the sound of movement as Joe dragged Tania to safety. They huddled against the wall, watching as the Russian shoved Paco toward the center of the room.

"*Everybody up! This is a fucking robbery! On your feet...*" Looking down at the guy playing X-box, he said, "*You too, fatso! Toss the gun over, or I blow his fucking head off. Hurry!*"

The fat man paused the game, dropped the controller then slowly pulled the gun from his waistband. Without taking his eyes off the Russian, he placed it on the ground and slid it toward him. The Russian retrieved it, awkwardly sliding it into his waistband while keeping his own gun on Paco. Then he looked back at the fat man, who was still staring.

"The fuck *you* looking at, pig-fucker?"

The fat man just smiled.

Next, the Russian turned his attention to the men on the couch.

"You two – on your feet. Don't make me shoot him. Hands in the air, c'mon... quick, quick!"

From their vantage point, Tania had an up-close view of the Russian. She could see that his hands were trembling and he was bathed in sweat. Even his voice sounded tremulous, whiney rather than commanding. She realized the Russian was dope sick, scared and desperate. By contrast, the dealers seemed calm and collected... as if it was just another day at the office. Even Paco, who had a gun pressed against his temple, seemed entirely nonplussed by the situation. The men moved with a kind of lizard calm, slowly and deliberately complying with the Russian's instructions, seemingly waiting to the opportunity to make their move.

The Russian seemed too scared and too desperate to actually pull this off. This wasn't some well-thought-out, meticulously planned heist, Tania mused. It was a half-cocked, spur-of-the-moment clusterfuck. This was the actions of a desperate, dope sick junkie and it was unlikely to end well. She closed her eyes, hoping that the dealers would at least be able to end this farce before anybody got hurt.

"Good..." the Russian said. "Now, you fuckers – up against the wall."

The men lined up silently. They stood in silence, holding their palms up as they stared at the Russian, seemingly committing every aspect of his face to memory.

It was the man with the goatee who finally spoke. "You really fucked up," he said. "I hope you understand that, homie. You fucked up *so bad*, right now. I almost feel sorry for you, man."

"Shut up... just shut up! Fucking beaner!"

"You got any idea who you're robbing, dumbfuck?" The goatee was chuckling now, relishing the Russian's creeping unease. "You're robbing *18th Street*, man! I mean, Jesus Christ... Nobody has ever been dumb enough to try an' rob 18th Street, man! You gotta be the stupidest motherfucker in the entire country, homes. When they get their hands on you? They gonna cut off your balls, man. Seriously – they're gonna cut them off and fucking *feed them* to you."

The others began smiling at this, enraging the Russian further.

"Shut up!" he screamed, his voice rocketing up an octave. "One more fucking word outta you an' I'll shoot him. Then I'll shoot *you*. Yes??"

"Whatever you say, man..." the goatee said, shrugging. "I'm just tellin' you how it is..."

The Russian scanned the room, eyes falling on Joe and Tania.

"You. On the floor..." Tania looked up and their eyes locked. "Yes, Im talking to *you*, fucking... stuck-up bitch. Get up."

Tania stood slowly and said, "Okay."

The Russian smiled, nastily. "Ain't too good to talk me *now*, huh bitch? Listen to me. You gonna get up and get the shit on the table for me. Slowly. No sudden movements."

Tania nodded.

"Now, bitch! Go on - pack up the dope, all the fucking dope. Put it in the shoebox with the money. Hurry!"

She glanced down at Joe, who mouthed, "It'll be okay." In the moment, she believed him.

Walking to the table, Tania quickly collected all

the colorful balloons together and dumped them in the shoebox. Then she placed the lid on top, before bringing it over. She stopped a few feet from the Russian. She realized she needed to piss badly and a mad urge to laugh came over her. She fought it back. She watched the Russian's hand trembling wildly, the muzzle of the gun twitching against the young kid's temple.

"Now what?" she asked.

"Hand it to this motherfucker."

Tania came closer, holding the box out to Paco. Paco stared at it for a moment, before reluctantly taking it from her.

"Now fuck off," the Russian said. "Back over there."

Tania scurried back over to Joe, and crouched down with him again. As they huddled Joe could feel her trembling. He whispered, "It's gonna be okay. I'm sorry, Tania."

"It aint your fault."

The Russian sniffed, more and more snot dripping down his face. "Okay. Okay, that's good. This is what's going to happen. Me and my friend here are going to go down the stairs, slowly. If anyone even peeks their head out of the door before I'm out on the street, I shoot him. No bullshit, I killed many men back in Russia. You do it once, after is no big deal. I'm no fucking joke."

With that, he poked the gun harder against Paco's temple, "Start walking, motherfucker."

Paco remained silent, looking over to the others for cues. The Russian shoved the gun against his skull again. "Don't worry about them. Worry about getting shot."

Paco's face was a mark of blind hatred, but he did as

he was told. As Paco walked toward the door with the shoebox clasped to his chest, Tania saw the Russian begin to tremble. He took a sharp intake of breath, seemingly fighting back a sneeze. Then, all at once, everything went to hell.

"*Ahhh... CHOO!*"

As the Russian let out a loud, wet sneeze, the gun went off – BANG! - sending the contents of Paco's skull exploding from his head. A glorious eruption of jellied brain matter and shattered bone fragments hit the wall, like some ghoulish Jackson Pollock drip painting. Paco fell to his knees. The top half of his face was gone, but he was still clutching the bloody shoebox to his chest. Then he slowly toppled over.

Tania's eyes moved from Paco's twitching corpse up to the Russian who was standing over him. His bewildered face was slick with blood and brains and he seemed to be trying to say something. His mouth formed a series of shapes, but no sound came out. His eyes fell on Paco, then moved to the murder weapon in his hand, eyes widening as if noticing it for the first time.

He looked at Tania in a pleading manner, as he finally got the words out.

"I didn't..." he babbled. "It wasn't... I mean, I didn't..."

As he stammered, the other men were making their move. They stalked toward him, with the sinister grace of panthers. Sensing the movement, the Russian spun to face them, waving the gun in their direction. They froze in place, three sets of eyes trained on him. The Russian's hand was shaking wildly.

"You're a fuckin' dead man," the goatee said. "You shot my *cousin*, you dumb motherfucker!"

He went to move forward, but the Russian screamed for him to stop, jabbing the gun in his direction angrily. The goatee stopped moving.

"Just.... just fucking.... Let me THINK, goddamnit. Fucking SHIT, man. Shit!"

The Russian mumbling to himself, seemingly weighing up his rapidly declining options. Tania thought he might be crazy enough to try and make a run for it. She looked at the door, estimating how long it would take before he got to it. Could he move faster than the others?

"Right," the Russian said, eventually. His voice sounded steady, confident as if he had decided on the right plan of action. "Let's fucking *do* this."

Then the Russian smiled disconcertingly, rolling his neck and eliciting a series of sickening crunches. When he returned his gaze to the men, Tania noticed that the Russian's hand was no longer trembling. Sensing the strange change in demeanor, the goatee raised both hands palm up and took a step forward.

"OK, man – let's not do somethin' stupid..."

His words were cut off by the Russian's bullet. It hit him in the throat, sending a graceful spray of crimson into the air and reducing his words to wet, guttural gurgles. His hands went up to his throat as he sank to his knees, eyes bulging in confusion and anger. As the blood began seeping through his fingers, he toppled over. The Russian fired two more times. The first bullet hit the fat man in the thigh. The next hit the mustache between the shoulder blades as he turned to flee. Both men went down screaming and bleeding and thrashing about. The Russian walked calmly over to them, dispatching them at close range. It ended with the sound of an empty chamber, but it didn't matter – they were all dead. A deep, heavy silence settled over the room. The Russian stood over the men he had killed, silently switching out the empty gun for the one he'd taken from the fat man.

Then he walked over to Paco's corpse and calmly pulled the shoebox from his grasp, tucking the blood-splattered thing under his arm. On his way to the door, he hesitated as if suddenly remembering that Joe and Tania were still there. He looked over at them. His expression, Tania thought, seemed almost pitying.

"Get up," he said.

Joe and Tania scrambled to their feet. The Russian's expression was unreadable as both sides regarded each other. Finally, Joe spoke.

"We didn't see nothing, man," Joe said. "Not a thing. Me and my old lady... we just wanna get the fuck outta here. I swear to you, you won't ever see or hear from us again. Cool?"

The Russian nodded, contemplating this. Then he gave them a *what the hell* shrug and repeated, "Cool."

Tania allowed herself to exhale. Then Russian opened fire. Three bullets hit home and a fourth went wild, as Joe and Tania collapsed over each other in a pile of bloody, tangled limbs. The Russian gave one final look over the carnage he had wrought before sprinting out of there, dashing past a baffled pair of junkies who'd been waiting on the stairwell. They watched him tear down the stairs two at a time, like a man with the Devil itself close on his heels.

* *

"I'm sorry," Tania said.

"What're you sorry about?"

"Peeing. I peed in my fuckin' pants, can't you smell it? It's probably on your upholstery. I'm so... *ugh*."

"It's alright. Don't sweat it."

They were in Joe's car, heading back to Hollywood. Smoking cigarettes with still-trembling fingers. It wasn't shock or fear that made their hands tremble, it was something different and unexpected. Something that felt like the aftermath of a particularly strong orgasm or the first, mind-blowing hit on the crack pipe, that hit which rocks your world so profoundly that most spend the rest of their lives trying to chase it.

"What the fuck just *happened*?"

Joe looked over to Tania, but she didn't answer. She just carried on smoking, languid and satisfied for a moment, before looking down impassively at the gaping, bloody bullet wound in her chest. She shook her head slowly and said, "Fucked if I know."

"I mean," Joe said in a voice that was a mixture of horror and wonder. "Just *look* at me!"

She looked at Joe, eyes widening in horror when she saw the extent of his injuries. As he drove one-handed, Joe pulled up his shirt to reveal the pair of bullet holes that had torn into his body. His jeans were soaked through with blood. All she could say was, "That's fucking *wild*, dude."

"Tania..." Joe asked, dropping the shirt. "Did we just *die*?"

Tania half closed her eyes and let her head rest lazily against the passenger window, as they made the turn on Ivar.

"I don't know, man. All I know is that I don't *feel* dead. If anything I feel..." she drifted off, a wan smile on her lips.

"*Amazing*?" Joe asked, quietly.

"Yeah..." she said. "I feel fucking *amazing.*"

They finally made it to The Gilbert Hotel. Tania's room was a run-down box with threadbare brown carpeting and a broken television bolted to the wall. They hurried past the front desk, Joe holding his insides in with his forearm, but the old Bangladeshi man behind the Plexiglas window with the NO GUESTS NO EXCEPTIONS sign pasted to it didn't look up from his newspaper.

Tania bolted the door behind them, nodding to the bathroom.

"I got works in the makeup bag," she said.

A moment later, Joe was perched on her bed, busily cooking up a generous hit of dope in a bent, carbon-scarred spoon. Before he started, he'd taken his shirt off to wrap around his abdomen like a makeshift bandage but the blood kept soaking through.

"I think I'm bleeding on your bed," Joe said.

"Don't worry," she answered, eyes glued to the bubbling brown liquid in the spoon. "It's seen worse."

He dropped a cigarette filter into the solution as Tania rummaged through the bag and cursed. She pulled out a single disposable syringe, still in the wrapper.

"Last one," Tania said. "I haven't used in months. You can use it first if you want..."

"Ladies first," Joe said. "So long as you don't have Hep C or fuckin' HIV or somethin'?"

"No," Tania said.

Joe looked down at the blood-soaked shirt wrapped around his gut.

"I guess it wouldn't matter at this point," he said. Tania smiled, conceding the point.

"Would you mind... hitting me? I'm shaking."

Joe shrugged and began unwrapping the 28 gauge ½ cc insulin syringe. She watched as he drew some of the caramel-colored mixture into it.

"Jesus Joe. That's a lot... I haven't had a fix in over a year..."

Joe raised an eyebrow. "Worried you're gonna OD?"

Tania tied off and presented her arm to Joe. Even after months away from the needle, her veins were still pretty screwed up. Getting a register would be tough for most, but Joe was an expert. They nicknamed him The Doctor on account of his way with a syringe, As his old running partner, Sal MacKenzie, used to say: "That boy could hit a vein in a goddamned mummy."

After a moment of gentle prodding, black blood blossomed in the syringe and Joe lovingly pushed the hit home. After she got her fix, Tania lay back on the bed, waiting for that familiar rush to hit. As she did, she watched Joe shoot up with all the practiced efficiency of an old timer. It came, right enough, but something was different now. The rush from dope seemed pretty anticlimactic after experiencing death in all of its terrible, wonderful glory. It reminded Tania of when she had smoked crack for the first time. How alien the idea that she could ever just *snort* coke again suddenly seemed. It was instantly rendered pointless, a monstrous waste of drugs.

Joe withdrew the spent syringe and flopped down next to Tania. As they lay there, they realized intuitively that something about them had been irrevocably altered. A new day was dawning for Joe and Tania.

*

4 days later, Joe was alone and lying on the floor of his basement apartment on Normandie and Franklin. He was puking yellow goo into a bowl already full to the brim with foul-smelling bile. He was shaking violently. His guts were hastily held together with layer upon layer of Ralphs Drugstore bandages and duct tape, and each time he retched he became paranoid that they would rip apart and his insides would come spilling out again. The phone rang. He looked at the digital clock, glowing on the cable box. It was 2:30 am. He crawled over and retrieved the handset.

"Yeah," he croaked. "Tania?"

"Joe? Oh God, Joe..."

"Yeah.... I'm here."

"I'm sick!" She sounded like she was crying, gasping for breath. "I'm fucking sick. I don't understand it. It started last night. It's getting worse... I bought a bottle of fucking methadone... drank the lot... it didn't even help..."

He listened as she vomited. He tried to sound comforting, shushing her gently until her convulsions receded.

"I know... I know... I shot some dope two hours ago, it didn't do a thing. I can't get this sickness to go... I've never been this sick... Never..."

They both listened to each other groan and sigh over the phone for a while. Their pain seemed to eventually give away to an exhausted surrender to the futility and horror of it all.

"Joe. I'm coming over. We need to get straight."

"OK."

Joe gave her directions. By the time he was done, he was panting with exertion.

"Gimmie twenty," she said.

45 minutes later she stumbled out of a cab and staggered toward the apartment building. She pounded frantically on Joe's door. As lights in the neighboring apartments started to blink on Joe wrenched it open. He was stooped over, like a little old man. She pushed her way past him.

The apartment was dark. Tania caught the smell of rotting meat. She couldn't tell if the smell was from Joe's apartment, or if the stench was emanating from the fetid wound in her chest. They embraced painfully.

"How're we gonna do this?"

"The bathroom…"

Tania let her heavy coat fall to the floor, exposing a David Bowie shirt, soaked crimson with seeping blood. She staggered after Joe. The fluorescent lights momentarily burned her eyes. Joe was standing there, pointing to the bathtub. It was full of water. An extension cord snaked in from the living room. An ancient 12-inch black and white TV sat on the lid of the toilet.

"This'll be the easiest way," Joe said. "The quickest, too. And it won't make a mess like the fuckin' bullets did."

"That's smart."

As if to emphasize the point Tania pulled off her t-shirt. Right between her tits in the space where the bullet had gone in was a wad of surgical cotton the size of a fist. It was stuffed into the wound and stained a gruesome shade of brown. It was clumsily held in place with peeling duct tape.

"I'm still scared," she said.

"I know."

"I mean, what if we don't come back this time? Or what if we do, but it doesn't *fix* us?"

Joe shrugged. "Could it be any worse than feeling like this?"

"No. I guess not."

Joe and Tania undressed silently. There was no embarrassment. After all, there is nothing two people could ever share more intimate than death. They folded their clothes into neat piles and placed them by the sink, grimly focused on the task at hand. Tania went in first. Joe held her hand as she climbed into the lukewarm water. She sat at one end of the tub with her knees pressed tightly together. The water began to turn pink. Joe gingerly eased himself into the tub after her.

Joe's bandages soaked through quickly. The bathwater steadily deepened from pink into a murky scarlet.

"Does it hurt?" Tania had a look of almost motherly concern on her face when she asked this.

"Not the wound. Everything else hurts, but not the fucking wound."

"Fucking same thing here."

Joe reached over and flicked the TV on. A rerun of Entertainment Tonight. Some stuffed suit was talking about some vacuous starlet's latest legal woes.

"Change the channel, Joe. If we don't come back, I don't want this shit to be the last thing I hear."

Joe flipped it to a shopping channel, where a woman with too much makeup and a stiff helmet of liquored hair was extolling the virtues of some hideous pastel-colored pantsuits. "*This truly is your all-in-one outfit, you'll exude confidence and grace whether you're in the office, or the checkout at Walgreens... I'm hearing the*

XXXL of the wintergreen, blush, and tangerine are already in limited supply..." Joe turned the volume down.

"Ready?"

Tania nodded.

Joe picked up the TV and

Dropped

It

In

The

Tub

ZZZZTTTTTTTT!!!!!!

There was a flash of intense white, a strobe-like flicker, the smell of ozone... and then nothing. The apartment building was instantly plunged into darkness.

And then it was over-

In an endless, soundless wave-

Ohm.

Joe came out of it first. The house was no longer shrouded in darkness and somewhere in the distance was the flashing of the microwave clock, which had been reset. The air smelt funny. In the dark, Joe could see the television floating in the water between them. The water was brown and fetid. They had shat themselves at the moment of death. It didn't matter. Nothing mattered anymore. Tania started to stir, lifting her chin from her chest, slowly. Joe smiled a slow, satisfied smile.

"How do you feel?"

Tania sighed, a long, ecstatic sigh. "Fucking fantastic. Got a cigarette?"

Joe placed a hand on his hair and it felt brittle, singed. But the unbelievable relief that he felt was better than any high, any feeling he had experienced up until now. As they both sat there in a tub full of electrified water and shit, coasting on their high, they started to slowly nod off into a gentle dream state. Things were finally okay again. Until the next time, at least...

• •

"My name is Joe and I'm an addict."

"Hi, Joe."

"I'm finding it impossible to quit. I've had 3 relapses in as many weeks. I know they say to 'keep coming back' but... I'm sick right now. It's been 2 days since my last relapse. I'm here because it's all I can think to do..."

As Joe talked, Tania sat next to him, watching. This morning as he lay passed out on Valium, she'd silently crept into the bathroom and looked at herself in the mirror. Withdrawal sweat was soaking every inch of her stick-thin body. Her tits looked a cup-size smaller. She thought of those awful pictures of Nazi concentration camp survivors. The hole in her chest wasn't healing. It was starting to smell worse and no matter what she stuffed in there – cotton, old newspapers – the smell still leaked out from under her clothes. She had even tried placing one of those air fresheners that cab drivers hang from their rearview mirrors inside the rotting cavern, but the uneasy mixture of decay and potpourri was somehow worse.

What use was this if the body couldn't heal itself afterward? She had been shitting blood for 4 days since the last reckless, desperate fix. She had gulped down a bottle of drain cleaner in a moment of feverish madness. This morning with the sickness back worse than ever she *had* to do something about it. When she and Joe had vowed to detox, once and for all, she had meant it. Of course, she had! But things look different when the sickness is on you, howling through your bones like some great black wind. But Joe, fucking Joe.... he seemed to be determined to stick it out. Even worse, he was watching her mindful of any sign of wavering on her part. It was like being back in that fucking sober living house, she thought. Back to the miserable cycle of meetings, prayers, and self-denial. She couldn't stand it.

Joe could stick out his attempt at doing it cold turkey if that's what he really wanted. After all, she rationalized, how could she help him with his own detox if she was also incapacitated by sickness? If she could just be well enough to help him, then maybe he stood a better chance of actually sticking it out. *Then* she would detox. Her mind made up, this morning she had a fix without telling Joe. She carefully slid the kitchen knife up into the hole in her chest and stabbed around in there until she hit paydirt. With a quiet gasp, she felt her legs turn to jelly and the darkness swallowed her whole. When she came to on the bathroom floor, she felt so good that it took all of her concentration to seem as sick and miserable as she otherwise would have been, after Joe rolled out of bed.

Now Joe's words of pain and sickness washed over her as she sat next to him in an AA meeting later that day. Even the old timers, the lifelong drinkers with red noses, rotted teeth, and swollen livers looked at this bedraggled pair with a mix of pity and barely concealed disgust. "I'm going to try to beat this addiction."

"...And that's it. I'm going to keep going. I'm going to try and break this addiction this time. Thanks for listening."

Thanks Joe.

Keep coming back!

One day at a time!

Afterward, they walked back towards the Hollywood and Western Metro. The car had been towed after being illegally parked for 2 days.

"I feel like shit," Joe said. "I want to die."

"Yeah," Tania said, "Me too. It can't go on for much longer, I guess..."

Joe rounded on her. "You lying fucking *bitch*. You're high as a fucking kite. I saw it in your eyes the minute I woke up. Don't give me that shit."

"I'm not, high! Honestly, Joe!"

She reached out to him, but he shrugged her away. He walked ahead of her, down into the station. When she caught up to him he spun to face her, his face a mask of contempt and disappointment.

"Don't try and bullshit a bullshitter, Tania..." he said. "I can see it all over your damn face. You were nodding out in the fucking meeting. In the fucking *meeting* for Chrissakes!"

Down on the platform, Tania stood next to Joe feeling like a chastised kid. She felt guilty, ashamed of her weakness and her dishonesty. On the display, it said the next train to Pershing Square would arrive in one minute. She looked over at Joe. He was ashen. A droplet of sweat was forming on his nose. Even though the platform was pretty crowded, the people gave Joe and Tania the wide berth usually reserved for the dangerously insane, or the stinking homeless. A blast of stale air gusted through the tunnel as a train approached.

"Tania?" Joe said, in a quiet voice.

"Yeah?"

"I'm sorry."

She was about to say something, but at that moment, as the train roared into the station, Joe was gone. He jumped from the platform like a cat, straight into the path of the approaching train. There was a sickening thud as the train rushed past, pulling Joe...

The scream of brakes and the yells of shocked commuters echoed around the station as Joe vanished from view. Tania felt a spray of blood hit her in the face, warm and coppery. ... She looked to her left. Something pink and soft and glistening had hit a small Mexican woman in the face with the force of an open-handed slap. She stood frozen for a moment before letting out an awful, animalistic scream.

All at once, the platform exploded into frenzied movement as people ran around in confusion. The train had come to a grinding halt, with Joe's mangled remains visible on the coupler, the axle, and the wheels. Someone screamed for the police in Spanish. Gawkers ran to the edge to see the gore, only for one teenage boy to projectile vomit onto the tracks before being dragged off.

In the confusion, nobody noticed a silent and slowly decaying woman making her way off of the platform and up the escalator.

• •

She considered following Joe into the path of an oncoming train in the weeks that followed. He had finally done it; Joe had cheated the cycle of abstention, sickness, and relapse. As the sickness worsened,

Tania found that the quickest, easiest way to do it was asphyxiation. The biggest problem was that when she held the plastic bag tight over her head, and the heat started to build as she instinctively gasped for breath, the urge to tear the bag off was almost unbearable. It took several attempts before she was able to see it through for the first time. After that, Tania was a pro. Once you rode out those two or three minutes of panic, death came on slow and easy, like sliding into a warm bath. Instead of rotting wounds or a bleeding anus, she was left with a red face – the result of the blood vessels constantly erupting under her skin. But she looked no worse, she supposed, than some of the hardcore alcoholics she had met at the meetings.

But still, she did consider doing what Joe did. There was something enticingly simple about the idea of of just ceasing to be. There was no coming back from an accident of that magnitude. There was nothing left to come back *to*. Perhaps it was the only way of ending this awful half-life once and for all. The rush from suicide was becoming less and less, and the withdrawal symptoms only seemed to intensify with each passing week. The past few months she had become a ghost, a shell, something that existed only in the shadows, reduced to a feral state of pure animal need.

A month or so later, something happened that made her give up any lingering thoughts of following in Joe's footsteps, once and for all. These days, she often found herself in the quiet section of Griffith Park where they'd spread Joe's ashes. Alone, the silence was so profound that it was easy to forget that beyond this island of calm the noise and heat and filth of the city was waiting, a patient monster biding its time. She sat on the grass, all alone, watching as the sun began to sink beyond the horizon in stunning hues of red purple, and yellow. Everything was quiet and peaceful. She placed her hand on the grass, feeling its coolness against her palm. She closed her eyes to enjoy the sensation.

It was then, in this fleeting silence that she thought she heard it. It was quiet, so subtle as to easily be written off as the imagination, but as Tania sat there waiting, she caught it again. It was a little louder this time, carried on the soft evening breeze.

Tania...
Taaania....
Pleasssee.....
Pleasse...
Just one last fix...
And then I'll quit...
For goood....

She let the tears that she'd been unable to shed at the time of his last suicide finally come. They rolled down her cheeks as she finally began to grasp the true extent of Joe's hell. She imagined him being scooped into a cheap casket and shoved into the waiting oven, reduced by the roaring, violent heat to literal ash... a billion or so tiny fragments of carbon, some of which were sent twirling up into the air and the rest scooped into an urn... then dumped in this place, left to be carried here and there by the careless breeze.

She imagined Joe... a million fragments of Joe... being carried around the city, clinging to the underside of plants and trees, finding themselves lost in discarded beer cans or stuck in piles of fresh dog shit... Now she realized that every single one of those infinitesimal specks of what Joe once was *still* somehow burning with that terrible sickness, that unimaginable hunger, that awful and unquenchable thirst for relief. A billion fragments of Joe, scattered through the filth and the noise and ugliness of the streets, each fragment futilely screaming for relief, for the final fix that will never, ever come. Ssuffering from a sickness that would last from now until the end of time.

Tania stood stiffly, looking around. Then she closed her eyes and addressed the wind.

"Goodbye, Joe," she said. "I can't come back here again. I'm so fucking sorry. For all of it. But the truth is... I can't *help* you anymore. I've got my *own* habit to feed."

As the sky turned black, the heavy silence of Griffith Park was replaced with a steadily ebbing and flowing chorus of crickets, who chirruped and sang for most of the night, occasionally accompanied by a billion subliminal screams of hunger and despair.

2

FRIDAY NIGHT AT PACO'S CRACK HOUSE

Joanie took a hit from the primo, filling the room with the pungent smell of marijuana and crack cocaine. She was in Paco's crib. It was Friday night.

Paco was strictly business. He dealt; he didn't smoke. His old connection, Soledad DeMartinez, an ex-Juarez whore turned cross-border kingpin, used to tell him: *Selling is more of a habit than using.* Back then, Paco was just another green sixteen-year-old looking to make some quick money and escape his miserable home, so he didn't understand. Fourteen years later, Paco understood perfectly.

Paco's kid sister sat slack-jawed and saucer-eyed, rolling the crack pipe around while she moved the flame along it, trying to collect the residue caked to the glass. Paco took care of Maria far better than his parents had managed. They tried to put her in a home until Paco intervened, *Retrasada* was what their father called it: *Retarded.* All Paco knew was that she came out of the womb with that same unnerving blank expression on her face and seemed somehow disconnected from the world around her. She didn't walk until she was four and didn't say her first word until she was almost eight. She didn't cry when their father beat her, nor ask where they were going the night Paco woke her up and took her from the house. The only thing that seemed to pierce her placid veneer was the pipe: if he took it away, she whined and pleaded for it just like any other dope fiend. So Paco gave it to her. She smoked but mostly was content to obsessively clean the pipe, collecting every last bit of residue like it was some kind of meditative practice. Paco left her alone to her ablutions, no longer curious about what – if anything – was happening beneath that eerily still surface.

Friday night at Paco's place meant an influx of eager customers. Friday was payday. The majority came over the border in search of the mythical good life: fat wallets, full bellies, happy wives, and the opportunity to raise children as lazy, spoiled, and feckless as any gringo brat. The majority found themselves trapped in the miserable, relentless grind of working under the table for subsidence wages in a country where, it seemed, for every dollar earned two more were simultaneously pickpocketed. They smoked to forget the previous week's indignities and petty humiliations and, by Sunday, were penniless and despondent, ready to climb back onto the cross on Monday morning.

Watching Maria with an amused look was a woman in her early twenties, who looked a good ten years older. Joanie was what men like Paco referred to as a *strawberry*, one of the women who traded sex for crack. Originally from Arkansas, Joanie didn't speak much Spanish and mispronounced the few rudimentary words she had managed to pick up. They communicated in grunts and gestures and Paco's half-assed English. He knew enough to get by twenty, forty, sixty, bundle, rock, on my way, and of course, *No credit.* When they fucked, he whispered hard and urgent Spanish words in her ear, which turned Joanie on. She particularly liked the word he used for her pussy, the way it sounded. *Chocha.Cho-cha.* It sounded both poetic and childlike. She liked the word for ass, too. *Culo.* She normally hated the way guys always wanted to put it in her ass. *Don't guys like pussy no more?* But when Paco told her he wanted to do it, she didn't mind so much because of how it sounded. *Culo. Cool-oh.* It sounded sweet, kinda.

Knock-knock.

Paco ambled over to the door, looked through the peephole, and then slid the locks back.

Joanie eyed the pale, twitchy fucker who walked inside. He was thirty-something with shoulder-length black hair, greased tight against his skull. He had black jeans, a black leather jacket, and a black T-shirt to match the black look in his eyes. His eyes darted around the room, settling on Joanie. He broke into a disconcerting smile before bowing. It was a curiously old-fashioned gesture that intrigued Joanie further. She smiled and introduced herself.

"What's up? I'm Johnny."

"Wachooneed," Paco demanded, suddenly impatient.

"Eighty white."

Johnny peeled the sweaty Jacksons from a thick bankroll, which Joanie clocked right away. She watched the exchange of money and drugs, and when it was over, she patted the seat next to her. Johnny came to sit.

"Don't mind if I do," he said. "Hotter than hell out there."

He reached into his jacket, retrieving a well-used glass pipe. *Never leave home without it.* Perched on the edge of the seat, he packed a generous hit into the blackened Chor-Boy. His movements were practiced and efficient. Next, he produced a miniature butane torch. It was the type of instrument more suited to a fancy Frog chef finishing off a crème brulee than a crackhead taking a hit. Joanie smiles as she thinks this, watching Johnny go about his business. He hit the pipe gentleman-style, one pinkie finger in the air, looking for all the world like some fat cat lighting a pricey Havana. Joanie dug his technique. He didn't just have a fat wallet, she thought. This fucker had *style*. Joanie shuffled closer as Johnny threw his head back and exhaled a great cloud of smoke.

"Goddamn," he said.

He rolled his neck, eliciting a sickening series of clicks and crunches, before saying it again: "Goddamn."

"Long day?"

"They all are."

Maria had continued to smoke, unblinking and expressionless. Joanie and Johnny watched absently as a brazen cockroach crawled up her arm. It was the size of a small mouse, but she didn't seem to notice. Before it reached the shoulder, the thing stopped and regarded the room from its vantage point, antennae waving softly as if stirred by a summer breeze.

"Mother *fucker*," Joanie spat, lunging to knock the thing off. Direct hit. It spun through the air, bounced off the wall, and finished up on its back, legs twitching. Maria didn't react. Joanie looked from Paco to Johnny before saying, almost apologetically: "I fucking hate roaches."

Paco grunted and went over to the TV. Turned it on, sat down before it, and loaded up his X-Box.

Johnny holds out the still-smoking pipe to Joanie.

"Thank you, kind sir..." she says, reaching for it.

As she takes her hit, Johnny begins talking, almost to himself.

"When I was 6," Johnny said, "my best friend and

I killed a boy."

She exhaled. Her ears rang, but as she'd been smoking all afternoon, it didn't get her high. It helped avert the crash for a little while longer. That was enough.

She hands the pipe back. Gives Johnny a curious look.

"I'm interested," Joanie says. "Tell me more."

"He was maybe three years old. We took him, my friend and me from the local mall. Saturday afternoon in the suburbs. The place was rammed. We just... walked him away from his mom while she was looking through a sales rack. Took him right out of the mall. Down to the train tracks."

"Is that where you did it? I mean, where you killed him?"

"Yeah. There was a pile of bricks lying around. My friend hit him on the head with one. Hard. He was hurt but still moving. So I stabbed him in the throat with my pocket knife."

"Jesus Christ..." Joanie says. "That's *heavy*, man. Why did you do it?"

Johnny shrugged. From the look on his face, Joanie figured he'd been asked this plenty in his life. "Wanted to see what it would feel like, I guess."

Joanie nodded slowly. "So?" she asked.

"So what?"

"So what *did* it feel like?"

Johnny's face gets this thoughtful, faraway look. "Honestly? It felt kinda... cheap. Two dimensional. Like some bad TV program."

"What happened next?"

"We covered the body up with branches and shit. My friend, Frankie, had an asthma attack. Nerves, I guess."

"Did you get busted?"

"Big time. We were dumb kids. Not even smart enough to try and cover our tracks. There were 7 or 8 witnesses who saw us leaving with the kid. It was a small town, so people recognized us. We made the national news. It was a pretty big deal. We were tried in another state because they were scared we were gonna get lynched or some shit. Court-appointed shrinks, lawyers arguing whether we should be tried as adults, the works. Went on for months and months before they decided what to do with us. They put Frankie in a state hospital. I got kid prison. They locked me up until I turned 18. Then, they were meant to turn us both loose. State law. I was the only one who made it out."

"What happened to your friend?"

"I heard he turned queer in the nutward. His schitzo boyfriend stabbed him 37 times. He was, like, 15 when it happened."

"That's tough."

"Life's tough., I kept my head down until they turned me loose. It was a process. They changed my name. I used to be called Adam. Now I'm Johnny. After *Johnny B Goode*, you know?"

Joanie smiled wistfully. "You know, I think I'd like to change *my* name"

"Oh yeah? What would you change it to?"

Joanie thought for a moment and smiled.

"Champagne," she said.

"Champagne!" Johnny chuckled. "That's a total stripper name."

Joanie seemed flattered at this. "You *think*? Man, I've always wanted to dance, but..."

Johnny gave her an appraising look.

"What's stopping you? You could dance, baby!"

"You really think so?"

"Stand up."

Joanie stood and turned around slowly. The drugs had eaten away at her face. But she had good legs. Johnny was a leg man.

"A buddy of mine owns a club called Gold Diggers on the east side. He's always looking for new girls."

"You think he'd like me?"

"Sure, he would. As long as you ain't shy."

Joanie grinned a wide, red grin. "I ain't shy, Johnny. When?"

"No time like the present."

Joanie went over to Paco, still engrossed in *Grand Theft Auto: Vice City*. She bent over, putting her lips to his ear.

"Hey, Papi... I'm just going to see about a job, OK? *Mucho dinero, si?* Be back soon."

She kissed his neck. Paco grunted but didn't shift his gaze from the screen. Fucking dope fiend bitches were all the same. She'd be back. They always came back.

Joanie grabbed her shit and said, "C'mon, Adam."

"Johnny."

"Oh yeah. C'mon, Johnny."

They left Paco, poor mute Maria, and the cockroach still furiously trying to right itself.

It was getting dark. Blood-red LA smog strangled the streets. A makeshift food cart, where churros and tamales sat next to barbequed corn on the cob smeared with mayonnaise and chili powder. A crazy homeless woman walked up the middle of the street, barefoot and muttering to herself.

Approaching the food cart, Joanie noticed a small boy standing next to it. He was 5 or 6 years old. Barefoot and shirtless, he was playing intently with a wooden cup and ball.

As they got closer, the kid's eyes fell on Joanie. They were the deepest shade of brown Joanie had ever seen.

"Look at this cutie," she said, tugging on Johnny's arm.

Johnny stopped, looking at the kid. He made a non-committal noise.

"Kids love me," Joanie said, cooing at the boy.

Suddenly, the mother came out from behind the cart to grab the kid by the arm. As she yanked him away, Joanie heard her hiss, "Esa mujer es una visciousa!"—*That is a bad woman.*

Johnny took a few steps before looking back at Joanie. "C'mon," he said, irritated.

Joanie just stood there, watching the woman pull the child away. When she looked back, Joanie flipped the bitch off and mouthed, *Fuck. You.*

The air felt murky, alive with static electricity. Some kind of storm was brewing. Joanie trotted after Johnny, catching up with him.

Here they were in this city of suckers and scumbags. Everybody was on the prowl for something: drugs, money, pussy, it didn't seem to matter. Joanie supposed she was no different from anyone else. She just wanted her slice of the pie, after all. Who in the hell didn't?

"Hey, wait up..." she called after Johnny.

As she drew closer, she realized Johnny was singing. She recognized it as the song he took his name from.

"He never ever learned to read and write so well...

"But he could play that guitar just like he's ringing

a bell..."

"Go, go!" Joanie and Johnny sang in unison. "Go, Johnny, go! Go!"

Johnny winked at her and said, "C'mon, Champagne... Stardom awaits!"

Laughing giddily, she linked her arm around his, and they bopped down the street together, singing and giggling. It was Friday night in Hollywood, and somewhere up above their heads, the California sky was pregnant with possibilities.

3

THE SEVENTH OD

Hazel had been a beauty once upon a time, the kind of girl men fought over, and women whispered about in the whirlwind weeks leading up to senior prom. But that was another world... another life. Now, she hardly recognized the smiling girl with emerald eyes and ivory teeth preserved in amber, between the pages of her mother's photograph albums.. The slightest recollection of that long-ago girlhood in Weeping Water, Nebraska, filled Hazel with queasy, breathless anxiety.

Perched on Mike's lap, Hazel idly twisted and untwisted his long, greasy hair with her fingers. Mike was Hazel's old man, a once-aspiring musician turned idle these last few years. Tonight, they were entertaining a guy they'd bumped into over at the 3 of Clubs, who called himself Smooth. Smooth was cross-legged on the floor in a state of extreme focus as he carefully prepared a shot of cocaine in a bottle cap. They had allowed Smooth to fix in their pad in exchange for an introduction to his pill connection, who was currently on his way over. According to Smooth, this motherfucker was down in Tijuana most weekends buying thousands of boxes of Xanax, Vicodin, Viagra, Ambien, Klonopin, Dilaudid, Oxycontin, and Quaaludes from a crooked backstreet Farmacia. "This motherfucker's got boxes of 'em in his storage unit. No shit, I seen for myself... And it's all legit, none of that pressed, fake-ass shit."

Smooth grinned and purred, "I'm talkin' *real-deal-Holyfield*, you dig?"

Their apartment was small and shabby. The kitchen

consisted of little more than a sink, a hot plate, and an overfilled garbage can. The way the bathroom was situated meant that anyone in the living room had to listen to the strains and splashes of everything that went down in there.

As Mike and Smooth talked absently about the sorry state of LA's cocaine supply these days, Hazel got up and wandered over to the TV. She picked up the remote and clicked it on. *Intervention* was playing on A&E. This was a favorite of Hazel's. The concept of the show was simple: unwitting addicts agreed to be filmed by a crew for "a documentary on addiction," only to be surprised by an intervention. Each episode built to that final, dramatic showdown: would they or wouldn't they agree to treatment? Hazel was obsessed with *Intervention*.

"Sheeit," Smooth said. "I'm older than you. You shoulda seen what went down in the nineteen eighties, son! Back then, cocaine was *real* cocaine; they had it comin' straight from Columbia. None of that bunk Mexican stuff they're slinging downtown."

"Some real *Scarface* shit, huh?"

"Fuckin-A. Tony-fuckin-Montana man... fuckin' A. The whole west coast was swimmin' in the shit. It was a fuckin' *snowstorm*, you dig?"

"Shhh," Hazel said absently. "I'm watching my stories."

The men fell silent as their eyes turned to the onscreen action. A sobbing crystal meth addict called Krystal was sobbing, surrounded by a gaggle of family, friends, and a drug counselor.

"Krystal," the counselor said. "Will you accept this gift of treatment?"

There was a dramatic pause... then Krystal

mumbled, "Yes..." and there were hugs and tears of joy as she was bundled up and shipped off to a treatment facility in Boca Raton.

"Shit, dunno if Boca is the place for this bitch," Mike said. "They got *bocoup* meth down in Florida... Primo shit, too! Plus, the weather is fucking great, better than... where's this bitch from?"

"Michigan," Hazel said.

"*Michigan?*" Mike chuckled at this. "Hell, I'd take that ticket too."

"You know what they say... all this reality bullshit is just for the cameras. Ain't none of that shit *real*."

Hazel looked up at this, mouth twitching in distaste. "Of *course* it's real," she said. "Look at poor Krystal! She's *crying*. Look, that's her momma, Pam, right there. See, the big lady? She's crying, too. Ain't nothin' fake about *those* tears."

Smooth was a good twenty years older than either Mike or Hazel. The noise of the television irritated him, and he turned his attention back to the task at hand. He began sucking the cooked cocaine into a disposable syringe through a cigarette filter. Tufts of grey hair peeked out from under the brim of his greasy brown fedora. His brow was furrowed in concentration, cigarette tucked behind his ear.

As he flicked the syringe to dislodge any air bubbles, Smooth nodded at the dusty electric guitar propped in the corner and said, "You play, Mike?"

"Oh yeah. I play. I was in a band, we were real good too... but you know. There were problems. With some of the other guys, y'know? I'm... doing my solo thing now."

"Mike's real good," Hazel said without taking her eyes from the screen. "Much better than those jealous assholes he used to play with, right babe?"

"Fuckin' A.   I'm writing new songs and shit. Gonna get something new together, perform my *own* shit. How about you, Smooth? You play?"

"Sure... played a little rhythm guitar," Smooth said, shooting Mike a yellow-toothed grin, "Funky shit..."

At this, Smooth begins to make a curious *chuga-chuga* sound as if trying to emulate the sound of a wah-wah pedal.   Then he snapped his fingers and says, "Shit, I used to jam with Sly motherfuckin' Stone back in the day. No shit! Those were crazy times. And Sly is a crazy motherfucker! *Cray- zee!* What 'bout you, Mike? You more of a rock and roll cat, huh?"

Mike smiled. "Yeah."

The credits started rolling. Hazel flicked off the TV and said, "Mike's group was real good. They woulda been huge if they hadn't split up when they did. Too many... *volatile personalities*, right baby?"

"That's right."

Mike and Hazel were both cooking their shots as Smooth slid the needle into his arm. He loosened the belt, hitting blood before easing the shit in slow and gentle. Sliding the needle out, he licked the blood from the puncture wound and said, "God *damn*, that's some boss shit. You, uh, mind if I take a look, Mike?"

Mike grunted his consent as he drew his shot into the needle. Smooth ambled over to the guitar and picked it up, propping it on his lap. As Hazel probed for a vein, Smooth played some clumsy blues chords, muttering about being out of practice. His fingers felt fat and slow, and the cocaine was making his hands shake. The moment he started playing, the coke dragged his focus elsewhere. He wanted to investigate the apartment; he wanted to examine the pile of paperbacks in the corner, he wanted to talk about Ronald Reagan and the shit he and Noriega pulled down in Nicaragua back in the day, he wanted to go stand on his head and tell some dirty fuckin' jokes. *Yo momma's so fat... the bitch fell outta both sides of the bed at once!*

His racing thoughts were interrupted when Smooth spotted a photograph in a cheap frame that was sitting on top of the television. He walked over and picked it up for a closer look. The girl in the picture was blonde, with dark eyes and dirty cheeks. She was giving the camera a huge, gap-toothed smile and holding a melting ice pop. She looked to be 3, maybe four years old.

Smooth said, "Who's *this* cutie?"

Hazel had just slid the needle from her arm, and the orgasmic rush from the coke was already overwhelming her. After letting out a long, ecstatic sigh, she said, "That's Devon... my little girl."

"Where she at?"

"My mom's place," she said. "Fuckin' family court took her away from me after I got sent away the last time. It's real fucked up."

"Shit, I hear you. Bein' a parent's no joke. I got two of my own, they all grown up now."

"You see them much?"

Smooth shook his head, face stony.

"Their momma turned those kids against me a long time ago. Last I heard, my son was going to college, but that musta been, shit... 5 *years* ago, maybe? Guess he must have done graduated already."

The cocaine was making her heart do cartwheels in her ribcage. She found herself talking about Devon and how her mother made it almost impossible for her to have any kind of relationship with her. She heard herself talking about last Thanksgiving when she had gone back to Weeping Water to see them. How Devon had jumped up on Hazel, screaming, "Mommy! Mommy!" and held on to her neck for dear life. How she loved that little girl, and that little girl loved Hazel... But it didn't matter because her goddamned mother had stood over them the whole time with that dour, disapproving look on her face. Making snide comments all day and treating her own daughter like some unwelcome interloper. She heard herself telling him about the fight, the big fight that had been simmering between them all day until it finally erupted over a particularly painful turkey dinner. The glasses that were smashed, the plates of food thrown, and poor little Devon curled up under the kitchen table, struggling for breath in between her terrified howls and sobs. And she talked about the blow that Hazel landed across her mother's smug, self-righteous face. How the old bitch had just stood there, hand against her cheek, as if unable to believe Hazel had the nerve to do it. How her mother had hissed, "Get out..." and how Hazel knew, just from the way she said it, that this would be the last time either of them would be in the same room again.

The words tumbled from her mouth in a coke-numbed babble. When she was done, she stretched back and lit a cigarette. There was silence in the room for a moment before Smooth delivered his verdict.

"That's some fucked-up shit," Smooth said. "Fucking families, huh? Am I right, Mike? Huh?"

He cackled, and Mike high-fived him. Soon, the talk started up again. Mike was chuckling now, saying, "This is good shit, man. I'm fuckin' glad we bumped into you tonight, bro."

"Shit, I'm shocked I've never seen you guys before. Y'all are friends of Sheena, right?"

"Right. Friends of friends, kinda..." Mike ran a trembling hand through his hair. "When d'you say this friend of yours is supposed to get here?"

"*Soon*, baby. Shit, I've known this cat for years. He won't keep us hanging around..."

They carried on getting high with the grim determination that an intravenous cocaine session entails. Soon, they were beyond words, their jaws locked tight, their hearts pounding in their chests, the grim compulsion to feed every last crumb of the cocaine into their arms was all that was left. Mike locked himself in the bathroom and took a sputtering coke shit before wiping up and splashing cold water on his face. He stared at his reflection in the mirror. His asshole felt raw and tender. His eyes seemed to vibrate in their sockets; his vision was blurring in and out. Already, he could feel it starting, the gnawing pit of self-loathing and despair that inevitably began to swallow him from the inside out once the coke was running low. He knew that from this point on, the night would be about trying to keep the inevitable horror at bay long enough for Smooth's guy to arrive with the pills. Without something to knock him out, maybe he would be tempted to use a knife on himself again. His arms were a patchwork of self-abuse: needle marks, calcified veins, razor slashes, and bloodletting. How long, he wondered, before he just finished the job? Put himself out of his misery?

"MIKE! YO MIKE!! GET THE FUCK OUT HERE, MAN!"

Mike snapped out of his thoughts. He rushed out of the bathroom to find himself confronted with a disquieting scene. Smooth was crouching over Hazel, who was convulsing on the floor. She was twitching and shaking, grabbing at her crotch with twisted, bunched-up hands.

As she gurgled and flailed, the words came spilling out of Smooth in a terrified jumble.

"I didn't do nuthin', man, I swear... I just looked over 'cos she was making this funny noise an' shit, and I'm like, yo? Is this bitch okay? But suddenly – BAM! She falls off the fuckin' chair and starts shakin' like fuckin' James Brown, an' shit. Is this bitch fuckin' epileptic?"

"No, she ain't..." Mike grabbed the phone. "Fuck me, she's fucking OD'ing again. It's the coke. This is like the 7th fucking time this month, goddamn. Imma call the ambulance"

Smooth stood up. He was suddenly all business. "You calling *what* now?"

"An ambulance. It's cool, she's insured and shit."

"I don't give a fuck about her insurance, man! What about the COPS?"

"Man, the cops can't do *shit*... not unless some idiot invites them in. Look, Smooth - why don't you wait here until we get back? The pigs probably won't show, but on the off-chance they do? Just stay put and wait till they leave. Don't answer the door to *anyone...* except your pal."

Smooth looked doubtful, but that faded as Mike began counting off the twenties. It's always bad form to hand over the bread *before* the drugs have arrived, even when dealing with friends of friends. Under normal circumstances Mike wouldn't have trusted his own mother with his dope money, never mind some motherfucker he just met in a bar. But desperate time called for desperate measures.

"There's two hundred," Mike said. "I want Oxy, Ambien and Klonopin... Lemmie write it down for you."

Mike hunted for a pen as Hazel flopped around on the floor, making those awful slobbering noises. After he scrawled his order and shoved the Post-it into Smooth's hand Mike said, "I owe you one, man. There's some beer in the fridge, help yourself. Just please... *wait* for him, yeah?"

Smooth looked from Hazel to Mike and said, "Okay, man. Shit. I'll wait. Just... look after your bitch."

Mike gave Smooth a grateful smile, before dialing 911. Smooth watched at Hazel as she trashed about on the floor.

"Yes," Mike said. "Ambulance, please."

"That's some freaky-looking shit..." Smooth muttered, before heading into the kitchen for a beer.

"Yes, hello... Uh- huh... My girlfriend is having a seizure. That's right. Uh-huh... yeah, the address..."

Smooth sipped his beer as he tidied away the drug paraphernalia. He ignored the looks that the paramedics gave him when Mike let them in twenty or so minutes later. By the time they showed up the worst of it was over and Hazel was silent, lying on the floor in the recovery position. They checked her vitals and Mike told them her name.

"Hazel! Hazel! Can you hear me Hazel?"

Her eyes remained dull and unfocused. There was a lot of commotion as they put her on the gurney and started to wheel her out of the apartment. They left Smooth on the couch, cracking open his second beer. Mike followed them out to the street, watching as they loaded her into the ambulance. He looked up at their apartment window and there was Smooth, looking out. He gave Mike the thumbs up.

Mike sat up front with the driver as they sped through the pre-dawn streets, toward the Cedar Sinai emergency room. The driver was asking a lot of questions about what drugs Hazel had been using. Mike said, "I think she has been doing coke," but refused to say any more than that. They rode the rest of the way in silence, as the siren wailed and Hazel started to regain consciousness in the back.

In the sodium glow of the emergency room, Mike paced and waited for word. The waiting room had a smattering of desperate people lounging around, nursing wounds or waiting for news about friends or loved ones. They looked tired, beaten down by circumstance. Still jumpy from the cocaine, Mike walked outside and stood smoking a cigarette in the sultry 4am murk. The cops showed after an hour, asking the same questions they always asked. They wanted to see his ID but Mike had none. They stalked over to Hazel's bed to question her. They seemed harassed and disinterested, finally leaving without making too much fuss. At 6 am, Mike was allowed to come to Hazel's bed. It was separated from the others by a flimsy plastic curtain. In the next bed over, a man was calling for his mother in a small, plaintive voice. From somewhere in the distance a woman's sobs echoed off the uncaring institutional walls. Hazel was sitting up in bed. She looked up at Mike with sorrowful eyes and said, "Can we get the fuck out of here, please?"

They called a cab and rode in silence back to the apartment. The rising sun cast spectacular colors across the thick layer of smog blanketing the city. The smog looked beautiful, Mike thought, like something you might see hanging in an art gallery. Hazel said, "I think I'm hungry. Is there any food at home?"

"I think we have hot dogs."

"Will you cook me up a hot dog?"

"Sure, babe."

She looked a little sadder than usual this morning. She stared out of the window, and Mike watched the light bouncing from the angles of her face. Mike said, "What's up?"

"It's just, I dunno..." she said eventually. "When I was stuck in that hospital bed and the doctors were poking me and looking at me like I was some fucking piece of shit... I got to thinking. Like, what's the point, you know? I mean, what's the fucking point?"

She looked at Mike. He stared back, expressionless.

"Look at that bitch on *Intervention*," Hazel said. "She didn't OD. She didn't wind up in the emergency room. She didn't even shoot up, for Chrissakes!"

She searched Mike's face for a clue that she had landed a direct hit, but he just shrugged and said, "So what?"

"So what?" Hazel bit her lip. "So... so why was *she* on TV? Like, what's so special about *her*? I just feel like... why am I putting myself through all of this shit when there's nobody even watching it all?"

Mike stared out of the window without speaking.

"I mean, shit, my mom... I know that she hates me an' all, but couldn't she have at least cared enough to call the show? One fucking phone call? I can't call 'em myself. I'm not supposed to know it's a set-up, you know? I mean, I'd play along! I'd act surprised when they did the intervention. I'd pretend that they were just doing some film about a fuckin'... day in the life of a drug addict, or whatever. I could do that. I just feel like... it's all being wasted, you know? All of this STUFF is happening... but there's NOBODY to SEE IT."

"I don't get you, babe. *Who* should be seeing *what*?"

Hazel let out a long, exasperated sigh.

"PEOPLE, Mike! I mean PEOPLE should be seeing ALL of THIS. People on the other side, you know?" she tapped the window for emphasis. "On the other side of the screen? The people watching at home."

Hazel stared out of the window sadly, as the city sped past.

"I just feel like I could be someone. I mean, really BE someone. But instead, I'm just wasting it all, here. What is the point of going through all of this, of feeling this, of hurting this fucking bad day in and day out... what's the point of all this fucking *pain* if there's nobody there to see it? If there's nobody watching... nobody making it *real*?"

"But it IS real. We're... real people, Hazel. Y'know?"

"No! No we're not. If nobody is WATCHING, how can it be REAL?"

They pulled up at the apartment. Mike paid the driver and helped Hazel onto the sidewalk. They trudged up the stairs and he slid the key into the lock. Stepping inside, the first thing Mike noticed was the silence. Smooth was gone. In fact, a lot of things were gone. The place seemed more chaotic yet somehow emptier than he remembered it.

"Oh shit," Mike said. "That low down, dirty

motherfucker."

Mike walked around the apartment in silence, hoping against hope that somehow amid the chaos he would find the pills he had paid for. Hell, if Smooth had left as much as a couple of lousy Valium then he could have forgiven the prick. Of course, Smooth had not left anything behind. The last of the coke, as well as the hidden stash of ketamine and crystal meth Mike kept tucked away in a hollowed-out hardcover copy of *The Collected Short Stories of Arthur C Clarke* was gone. The bastard had even taken their copy of *The Complete Pill Guide For Nurses*. Mike's guitar was gone. The kitchen drawers hung open, emptied of their meager collection of silverware. In the bedroom Mike looked at Hazel's underwear drawer, hanging open, emptied of most of her panties.

"That fucking piece of shit robbed us. I'm gonna kill him. I'm gonna cut his fucking throat when I catch up with him."

"He left the TV," Hazel said, as she walked over and sank to her knees before it, reaching for the remote control. "At least he left us the TV."

Mike stalked around the apartment, kicking things and cursing to himself. Every so often he would notice something else missing, and scream out their name – *my Fugazi records! My skull ring! My fuckin' DVDs!* – a roll call of despair and fury. Hazel was calm, watching the television with a curiously blank expression, the cathode light making her pallor seem less pronounced.

"I'm *hungry*, Mike." she said. "They pumped my stomach back there, will you make me some hot dogs now?"

"Okay, okay... Shit," Mike grumbled. "One sec."

Mike walked over to the fridge. He wrenched it open and stood there, staring into it for a moment, seemingly uncomprehending. The goddamned fridge was empty. That lousy motherfucker had even emptied out their goddamned *fridge*. All that was left behind was a tub of expired sour cream and a half stick of butter.

"He stole the fucking hot dogs," Mike said, matter of fact.

Hazel didn't look up.

"Babe? Did you hear what I said? That bastard stole the fucking hot dogs."

Outside their window a police siren wailed and a homeless woman cursed and shrieked at the passing traffic. Somewhere a car alarm started up, playing a hypnotic melody that weaved around the woman's screams like an Ornette Coleman countermelody.

"Shh," Hazel said, without taking her eyes from the screen. "I'm watching my stories."

4

WAITING FOR CJ

I was walking up the winding street toward CJ's place, dope-sweat soaking my T-shirt and underwear, breathing ragged under the unforgiving sun. Los Angeles was not designed with pedestrians in mind. I heard the crunching gravel of an approaching car. I stepped aside to let a black Volkswagen Jetta pass. It slowed up, and the window rolled down to allow the passenger to aim a great gob of phlegm at me. It splattered on my jeans as the car sped off, kicking up dust. As it disappeared around the curve, I heard the spitter scream, *"Fucking bum!"*

his kind of shit happened whenever I traversed Los Angeles on foot. Non-car owners were typically regarded with scorn and suspicion. This neighborhood wasn't the Hollywood Hills, but a slick realtor might call it *Hollywood Hills adjacent*. I lived much further down the hill, in a dilapidated room of *The Mark Twain* - a transient hotel on the shitty end of Hollywood Boulevard. CJ, for as long as I'd known him, had lived up here. His folks were were not rich, but they were wealthy enough to pay the rent on this place, give him a small allowance, and bankroll his regular stints in rehab.

Last night, CJ and I heard that Lilly OD'd. Lilly was a junkie whore and petty thief we knew from the methadone clinic. Her regular connect was Gordo, who operated down by the Pico-Union. Hearing that Gordo was selling shit strong enough to kill a chronic dope fiend like Lili, we immediately set up a buy. When I got to his place, CJ would drive us downtown to score a bundle of this killer dope with the money we'd pooled. We fantasized idly about stepping on it for resale, making moves in the cut-throat world of the Hollywood dope scene, and maintaining our habits via a coterie of loyal junkie customers. We both knew, deep down, that we would instead gorge ourselves until every last crumb had been fed into our veins. My days with CJ had followed a familiar pattern since we first met at the methadone clinic on Hollywood and Cahuenga: countless long, languid Los Angeles afternoons spent in the deadly-serious pursuit of temporary oblivion.

For the past three years, CJ has been my best and only friend in this whole fucking world. I first clapped eyes on him while waiting in line for my daily dose of the sweet green stuff.

It started with a commotion at the dosing window. I craned to see CJ banging on the counter and demanding to 'speak to the manager' like he was in some fancy Beverly Hills restaurant instead of a grotty government clearing house for drug casualties. He was tall and skinny, all black leather and denim, with a pair of oversized 60s wayfarers pushed up into his thick, greasy black hair. He looked like Keith Richards' younger, sicker, somehow even-more fucked-up cousin. He went on about his human rights and threatened to call his lawyer over some perceived slight. It wasn't what was happening that caught my attention, however. It was what DIDN'T happen that was so unusual. The clinic routinely had troublemakers tossed out by security and banned from the premises. Perhaps it was his air of authority or the legal jargon he threw around, but CJ had the bastards going. Someone old and harassed came hustling from the back office, trying to mediate because, despite his degraded condition, it was obvious that CJ was well-educated and perhaps monied. Soon, he had the old guy tied into rhetorical knots. Not that it was difficult to outsmart the staff in this place. They were a motley crew made up of the kind of hateful, mental subnormals that even the officious sadists of the DMV would think twice about hiring.

I didn't see how it all played out, but CJ's proud and feisty demeanor in the face of the clinic's dour officialdom made an impression. I lingered in the parking lot until CJ finally emerged. Our eyes met, and he came over to bum a cigarette. We were inseparable from that moment on.

CJ was my best pal and a fountain of all kinds of useful knowledge. He taught me the art of the 'spit-back' – the trick of regurgitating your methadone on command to rebottle and sell. A bottle of spit-back methadone would net enough for a bag of shitty downtown dope. The secret was to make yourself vomit immediately before attending the clinic. "Gotta clear out the old pipes," as CJ put it.

It was CJ who taught me how to turn powder cocaine into crack with nothing more than some ammonia and aluminum foil, instead of having to fuck around with baking soda and microwaves. Or how to fashion a meth pipe from one of those glass pipettes they sell in certain bodegas, with a tiny fake bloom inside under the name *Romantic Roses*. You know, all kinds of useful shit. But despite these positive attributes, some of the other cats at the clinic didn't trust CJ.

"He's a fucking rich kid," Johnny D told me once, old black face wrinkling in scorn. "Soon as it gets too tough, all CJ has to do is call his folks, and they'll whisk him away from all of *this*." But I knew better than that. A born-to-lose aura hung around CJ; it clung to his hair and clothes like the stink of low-class motel rooms. He was no tourist; the dope scene was his life. There was no danger he'd run back to the old homestead if things got too tough. Things were *already* tough. He was losing his teeth, and money was tight. The allowance wasn't enough to support his dope habit, and CJ had to do plenty of nasty things to keep the money coming in since his folks stopped returning his calls. CJ was an expert shoplifter, but his real talent was with words. CJ's honied tones worked like a snake charmer's melody. Anyway, CJ came from money. That meant every two-bit dope peddler from Macarthur Park to Venice Beach wanted him in debt to them; they call that *The old ace-in-the-hole*.

But to me, CJ was that rarest of things in the dope scene. He was my *friend*. A genuine, won't open up your balloon and steal the dope out of it, kind of friend. The rarest kind there is.

I finally made it to his door, panting like a dog in the blazing desert heat. On the doorstep was the month-old jack-o-lantern, which had devolved into a pile of evil-smelling sludge, where a menagerie of fruit flies and other bugs congregated to feast.

I knocked and got no answer.

This wasn't unusual. CJ spent most of his life in a state of semi-catatonia, after all. I lifted the mat, which bore the legend *Fuck Off* in fancy, cursive lettering, to retrieve the spare key. I turned the key in the lock and pushed the door open.

As I stepped inside, I felt the sweat that had gummed my T-shirt to my back immediately start to cool. For a moment, it felt wonderful. Then I felt the gun pressing cool and hard against my temple, and a voice growl:

"Don't move - don't breathe - don't say a fuckin' word, cocksucker."

I froze, just like the voice said. *Oh Jesus,* I thought, *Please don't kill me now. Please don't let me go out dope sick.*

"You're not CJ."

The voice sounded disappointed. I started to instinctively turn my head, but a jab from the gun made me stop myself.

"I said don't *move*, asshole!"

"Sorry!" I took a deep breath before adding, "My name's Tony."

"What you doin' with a fucking key? You live here, too?"

"I used the spare." Getting no reply, I pressed on. "Officer? I mean, sir..? I don't know anything about whatever is going on. I was just checking if CJ was alright 'cause I hadn't heard from him in a little while..."

I felt the gun being lowered. My bowels loosened a little.

"I ain't no fucking cop, dummy."

As the gunman stepped out of the shadows, I felt a sickly jolt of recognition. He was short, caramel-skinned with a bushy mustache and a *Lakers* top. He wore a thick, yellow-gold chain and a filthy cap with a portrait of the Virgin de Guadalupe on it. A name came to me in a flash. "*The Cat in the Hat*," CJ had called him. "Good shit, but *a real fucking psychopath.*" The Cat who sold crack out of the projects in Ghost Town did not look like a happy camper.

"I guess CJ owes you money?"

"That's right. That shitbird owes me a *lotta* fuckin' money, and I'm here to collect."

"How did you get in?"

"How d'you think, asshole?" the Cat said with a humorless grin. "I broke in, fool."

The shock of having a gun pointed at me had started to recede a little, and my mind started whirring and evaluating. If I could somehow sweet-talk my way out of here, perhaps I could get to a phone and warn him. Those of us on the lower rungs of the junkie pyramid relied on beepers, and in junkie circles, an elaborate pager code had sprung up. Over the years, the meaning of 911 had degraded to near meaninglessness. Every dope-sick junkie waiting for a terminally late connection would start texting 911, which is why, between CJ and I, the code 999 was reserved for a capital-E emergency: overdoses, potential busts, or gun-toting dealers in your apartment.

"Well, now we've got that cleared up..." I held my palms out in a good-natured 'aw shucks' manner. "This looks like it's something between yourself and CJ. I gotta split, anyways... places to go, people to see, and all that. Tell him I was asking after him..."

I had made it a couple of steps toward the door before he gestured to the couch with the gun and said, "Sit your fuckin' ass *down*, pendejo."

I backed toward the couch with an ingratiating smile, practically bowing to the motherfucker as I babbled, "Suppose there's no *big* rush... might as well rest the old feet for a while."

"Just... shut the fuck up, for a minute! God-*damn.*"

I shut the fuck up, pulling an invisible zipper across

my lips for good measure. The Cat's eyes narrowed in suspicion.

"So you don't know where this cocksucker is?"

I shook my head. There was a long pause... before he shrugged and tucked the gun into his jeans.

"Then we gonna wait," he said.

The Cat perched next to me on the couch. I could sense him watching me as I thought about the gun jutting up into the small of his back. "Shit," the Cat said eventually. "This motherfucker doesn't even have a TV, man. Just a bunch of pendejo books."

He nodded to CJ's bookcase, teeming with all those great literary drunks and fuck-ups. Junk is a drug particularly suited to languid afternoons with your nose buried in a book, dreaming with your eyes open.

"Whatchoo say your name is?"

"Tony."

The Cat whistled thoughtfully. "How come you got a key to his place, Tony? You two fags or somethin'?"

This exchange was interrupted by the unmistakable sound of the toilet in CJ's on-suite bathroom flushing. My stomach dropped. So, CJ must have been here the whole time! The poor bastard was probably so engrossed in finding a working vein that he didn't hear any of this shit, utterly oblivious to the danger. I glanced at the Cat. Taking in my panicked expression, he just laughed.

"Don't worry, shithead," he said. "That ain't your boyfriend. Someone *else* is looking for this prick, too. Like I said, that cocksucker's in a lot of trouble, man."

The door to CJ's bedroom swung dramatically open, and an enormous black figure kinda...glided into the room.

"You have gotta be fucking kidding me," I said.

This motherfucker was tall, six and a half foot at least, with a black cloak covering his entire body and a cowl obscuring his face. Over one shoulder, he carried an ancient-looking scythe with a long, gnarled wooden handle and a malevolently sharp blade. As he glided toward us, I caught a glimpse into the shadowy folds of the cowl and felt the hairs on my neck stand up. There was no getting around it. This motherfucker was Death himself, looking like he'd walked straight off of a tarot card.

"I AM DEATH," announced Death.

"Yeah, no fucking *shit*, you are!"

I turned to the Cat and mouthed *Is this guy for real*? The Cat nodded.

"You know, it's weird..." I said, looking at the apparition.

"I guess I didn't expect him to be so ... y'know ..." I suppose I figured Death wouldn't have such a clichéd look. It was the dawn of a new millennium, after all. Maybe I'd expected a modern makeover, like that shitty Brad Pitt movie I saw on cable. Most disconcerting, however, was the voice. It wasn't a voice that resonated with chilling power. It was cold, sure - you could visualize icy particles forming between words. It was the kind of insincere monotone more suited to a tech support drone or some slimy cable company sales dick, not a terrible emissary from another plane. And the capper? He had an American accent. Death was American, which made a kind of sense, I suppose.

Death sat opposite us. He was a man of few words; his breath sounded like the wind whistling through cobwebby pipes. I turned to the Cat.

"Hey, listen," I said with an ingratiating smile, "I'm kinda dope sick, man. I was only stopping by to see if I could borrow money offa CJ.. I'm meant to be meeting someone downtown, like, right now. This dude can get kinda... pissy if I'm late, y'know?"

"So fucking what?"

"It's just... If you want me to stay – and that's totally cool, whatever you say – I was thinking maybe, while we're waiting, you might be able to... y'know. Front me a little stuff? I hate to ask, but I'm *really* sick, man."

The Cat in the Hat shook his head in seeming disbelief.

"You're sitting between a pissed-off drug dealer and Death himself, homeboy, an' you're asking for *credit*? If I was you, I'd keep my fuckin' junkie mouth *shut*."

I tried to keep quiet, but it proved impossible in light of the situation. Questions tugged at my sleeve like a gaggle of persistent hawkers in an Arab bazaar.

"Um... so, hey there... Death? I was just wondering..."

The cowl turned toward me, and I sensed the infinite darkness beyond. "YES?"

"So.... what happened with CJ, man? I mean, you're here for *him*? Today, I mean?"

He silenced my nervous babbling with a wave of his skeletal hand.

"I AM TAKING HIM TODAY. OVERDOSE..." Death said.

"An overdose? Interesting..." I started to wonder if my old buddy CJ had OD'd because he made the buy from Gordo *without* me. As I mulled this over, my face darkened. *That's what the selfish prick gets,* I heard myself think. *Sneaking around and getting high without me.* I pushed the thought away. CJ was my best friend, after all.

"So..." I asked, "You're just going to sit around and wait here for him to show up... Then what happens?"

"I TAKE HIM," Death said. "I HAVE FOURTEEN MORE IN HOLLYWOOD TO SEE TODAY. YOUR ASSHOLE FRIEND IS MAKING ME LATE."

The Cat leaned forward, suddenly interested.

"Yo, D... there's one thing I don't get. Like, a million motherfuckers die every day, at least... right? So, how come you got the time to be sitting around in *this* prick's apartment, just waiting for him to show up? Don't you got other pendejos to ice?"

"DEATH IS LEGION," Death said with a touch of melodrama, "DEATH IS EVERYWHERE..."

"So, you're saying it's a done deal that CJ is gonna fuckin' overdose?" I asked. "Like...it just hasn't happened yet cuz he's running late?"

Death made a vaguely affirmative noise.

"And basically, CJ is as good as dead?"

"HE IS DEAD. HE JUST DOESN'T REALIZE IT. THE DIE HAS BEEN CAST."

I nodded slowly, then looked at the Cat. From his put-out expression, I knew he'd caught my drift. I grinned and asked him, "So... what the fuck are *you* hanging around for? Dead men can't settle debts."

The Cat spluttered indignantly. "Fuck that, homie! That motherfucker is into me for three-fuckin-grand. I ain't leavin' until that prick coughs up."

"CJ's already dead, man, Death is sitting right *there*. What are you gonna do – threaten him?"

I could see the Cat doing furious mental

calculations, his face darkening. He grabbed the gun and shoved me aside with it, addressing Death directly.

"Listen, Death... I ain't lookin' to start no shit with you. We're *cool*, homie. But this fool gotta point – I gotta get my money *first*. You can't be taking this junkie fuck until he pays what he owes. It's only fair, man."

His voice shot up at the end, making the final statement more of a question than a demand. I began chuckling.

"CJ ain't gonna give you shit! That gun ain't gonna scare him. Not with Death sitting in his fucking armchair!"

The Cat looked earnestly at Death. "Let's make a deal, man. Maybe you could... I dunno, split for a while? Just while I beat the money out of this prick. Then he's all yours."

"DEATH MAKES NO DEALS." Death pointed a long, bony finger at the Cat. "DEATH IS NON NEGOTIABLE."

I found myself enjoying the Cat's discomfort and started peppering Death with questions.

"So you know when everybody is gonna die, huh?"

"OF COURSE."

"Even me and this dude, huh?"

"EVERYBODY."

I mulled this for a moment before jamming a thumb in the Cat's direction. "So, what happens to *him*?"

"Mother-*fuck!*" The Cat jumped out of his seat as if trying to stop the question from landing, but it was too late. "HE DIES FROM A GUNSHOT WOUND IN TWO YEARS AND SEVENTEEN

DAYS."

The Cat seemed to collapse into himself at this for a moment before recovering enough to bleat, "Who the FUCK fires that bullet, man?"

"You can't ask that!" I protested. "That's like... against the rules or something. Right Death?"

"The fuck do *you* know about the rules, shithead?"

"He said death is non-negotiable. If he tells you, you could try and change it or some shit."

"Yeah, but..." the Cat trailed off as the various logical strands of this argument worked themselves into a Gordian knot. "Shit, man," I said with a sympathetic smile. "It comes with the territory, I guess. Tough profession."

"You better keep your mouth *closed*, dickweed. Otherwise, this dude might have two jobs to do in here."

"IT IS NOT HIS TIME," Death said. "HIS COMES SOON ENOUGH..."

The Cat broke into a malicious grin. "I'll fuckin' *bet*. What happens to this prick?"

"DO YOU *REALLY* HAVE TO ASK?"

I coughed and self-consciously rubbed the track marks on my forearms. Everybody's gotta go sometime, I supposed. If you're going to check out, at least check out doing something you love – that's my motto. A pensive silence fell over the assembled company. Pondering our fates, I suppose.

"Listen, Death..." The Cat said after a while, "Hear me out. I was here first... I mean, that's gotta count for *something*. Be reasonable, man... I have two little girls to feed."

"IT COUNTS FOR NOTHING," Death said. "AND YOUR FAMILY IS OF NO CONCERN

TO ME."

The Cat let out a defeated sigh before slumping back onto the couch. I gave him a nudge.

"Hey man, can I *please* go now?" I felt my guts knotting and knotting ominously. "I'm gonna shit my pants if I don't fix real soon."

"Shut the fuck up and stay put! We ain't done, homie." He turned to Death and pleaded, "Come on, man...there's gotta be something we can do. Let's make a deal..."

"Why don't you flip a fucking coin or something?" I asked, looking between Death and the Cat. "I'm fucking dope-sick! You understand? I need to get the fuck out of here and cop, like, *yesterday*!"

Death seemed to consider this.

"YOU ARE SUGGESTING... A WAGER? TO DETERMINE THE FATE OF THE JUNKIE?"

"Whatever you wanna call it, man!"

"The junkie cocksucker is talking sense," the Cat said. "I'm down if you are, man..."

"A GAME OF CHANCE TO DETERMINE THE FATE OF ONE YOU CALL... CJ," Death said, grandly.

"Fuck yeah, let's *do it*, homie..."

Death reached a bony hand into his robe and produced a fancy-looking game board covered in black and white squares. The Cat eyes narrowed to slits.

"What's the fuck, dude? You wanna play Chinese-fuckin-checkers?"

"THIS IS A CHESS BOARD," Death said, sounding irritated.

"Chess? Shit, I don't know how to play no fucking chess, homie! It's gotta be something we *both* know how to play..."

The Cat rummaged in his pockets before pulling out a pair of well-worn dice. "We're gonna shoot BONES, homie. *That's* my motherfuckin' game! Waddya say, D?"

Death nodded slowly, then turned to me.

"IS THIS AGREEABLE TO YOU?"

This caught me off-guard. "Me? Shit, I don't know."

"Yo," the Cat said, "Who gives a fuck what this faggot thinks? He ain't playing!"

Ignoring him, Death said, "AS YOU ALSO CAME TO THIS PLACE FOR CJ, SO YOU SHOULD ALSO HAVE THE OPPORTUNITY TO DETERMINE HIS FATE."

"This is bullshit," the Cat protested. "Total fucking bullshit, man. This is between you and me, D!"

Death nodded to me. "WHAT WILL IT BE?"

The Cat tapped me on the shoulder with the pistol. "You win, motherfucker," he hissed. "We're straight. Just get the fuck outta here before I change my mind."

"But he said I could play..." I said. "CJ is my best friend, man! I owe it to him to at least *try*..."

"Motherfucking junkie cocksucker," the Cat muttered, pulling something from his pocket and holding it up for me to see. It was a large baggie of rocky, off-white powder. There had to be a couple of grams of whatever-it-was, at least. I leaned in for a closer look, and as I did, the Cat began making his pitch.

"This right here is the real deal, Holyfield. I get it in special for a client. He's, uh... let's just say *well known*, a real high-roller. It's the only dope he'll touch, man. None of that bullshit Mexican black tar shit you fucking street junkies is shooting up. This comes straight from the golden triangle, man. This came outta some jungle factory, straight into some poor bastards asshole, and then direct to *me*. No cuts. No bullshit. Just 3 grams of pharmaceutical-grade, number 4 heroin. You don't even need to cook it; the shit just dissolves in the water. If you want it, it's yours..."

I reached for it, but the Cat yanked it away. "Nuh-uh-uh... If you take it, that means you're *gone*. Leave the games to the big boys."

I stared at the baggie hungrily. It all boiled down to a binary choice: CJ or the dope. A one-in-three chance to save my friend from a terrible fate or the certainty of a baggie of the kind of high-quality dope I had only heard whispered rumors of from the kind of ancient dope fiends who remembered the glory days of paregoric and opium tincture. A long-lost world where a man could get as high as he liked without some nosy motherfucker making trouble for him. A world that vanished forever once Harry Anslinger came along to found the DEA and fuck shit up for *everybody*.

I swallowed hard... As far as decisions went, it was no decision at all.

"Pleasure doing business with you," I said, pocketing the dope.

"Cool," the Cat said. "Now fuck off."

I got to my feet, giving Death a little bow and a little wave to Cat in the Hat.

"It's been a pleasure, boys..." I said. "Guess I'll see you around."

The Cat made a whooping sound and began shaking the dice in his hand, giving them a little blow for good luck. As I crept out of CJ's place, I heard them bouncing across the coffee table as the Cat screamed encouragement.

Outside, the sky was clear and brilliant. The world seemed utterly oblivious to the fate of my friend. I wondered absently who would win out. In a way, it didn't matter much. Death or death on credit were the only options CJ seemingly had to work with.

You may feel that my decision to take the dope seems somehow selfish, callous even. But the simple truth is this: when you've got a habit like mine, free will is an illusion. That's why I couldn't stay mad at CJ over his scoring from Gordo without me. Of *course* he did, the poor bastard. If the situation were reversed, I would have done the same fucking thing. It ain't right, and it certainly ain't *nice*... but it just *is*. I'm a junkie, and while I'm using, my habit is non-negotiable. This is the truth: love, honesty, a sense of morality, and all of that shit that determines a person's basic character is, for an addict like me, an unaffordable luxury.

The worst part of all? I can see my actions clearly, even as I'm doing the awful thing that will alienate my few remaining friends, make my mother cry, and inflict long-lasting, deep emotional scars upon the one I love most in all the world. The one who stuck by me when all others left, the one who repeatedly asked the unanswerable questions, *Why isn't my LOVE enough? Why do you always have to DESTROY everything?* The shame and the guilt and the self-hatred are almost unbearable, but there is no stopping it when the wheels are in motion. All you can do is try to file down the sharpest edges with more dope, more booze, more lies, more betrayal, more, more, more... Until one of two things happens. Either the day comes that you somehow manage to see the place where the road runs out fast approaching, and you have the forethought to slam on the breaks, make it for real this time, burn your old life to the ground, and finally have the balls to walk through the flames without fear or hesitation. To allow yourself to be reborn, naked, vulnerable - a shellshocked child in an adult's, half-knackered body. Or the day comes when you walk in on Death shooting dice with your crack dealer to decide who gets the pink slip for your rust bucket of a soul.

As I pondered the rights and wrongs of what had happened, I was stopped in my tracks by an incredible sight. It was someone's pet dog, one of those fruity, twitchy miniature numbers so popular around these parts. It was well-groomed and all trussed up in an ostentatious ruby collar, which had the name *Butch* spelled out in diamantes. Most likely, Butch had got free from the yard of some sickeningly rich Hollywood queen, who kept him on a diet of filet mignon and shrimp. Now that the pampered little bastard was out of his velvet prison, he seemed to be on some kind of wild, degenerate sexual rampage. I nearly tripped over Butch as he was up on his hind legs furiously fucking a dead skunk. The thing had been recently run over, so the contents of the skull were splattered all over the asphalt in a brilliant explosion of reds and purples while its withered tongue hung comically from the shattered jaw. Those glassy, expressionless eyes seemed to somehow still register this final indignity being visited upon it by Butch, who screwed the mangled roadkill with piston-like thrusts, all the while making these awful little squeaking noises.I was a few feet from this awful spectacle, unable to tear my eyes away, even as my repulsion grew. Jesus, Butch was really going at it, despite the baking desert heat. Suddenly, there was a blur of movement in my peripheral vision, something dark and fast that came flying out from a nearby dumpster. It took me a moment to realize that this blur was, in fact, a half-starved and rather mangy-looking coyote. Poor Butch, the dirty little skunk-fucker, was utterly oblivious to what was happening until it was too late. In a flash, the coyote was on him, and, with a terrible snap of its savage, drooling jaws it clamped down on Butch's neck. Then it began dragging him back to the dumpster. As I watched Butch go, I noted, with a shiver of revulsion, the poor bastard's tiny, bright red lipstick-like cock jutting out of his fur. Butch was too shocked to put up a fight, and allowed himself to be dragged off with an expression of dumb, animal amazement. For a moment, Butch's eyes met mine as if silently pleading for an intervention. Then, just like that, they were both *gone*. Only Butch's agonized yelps and whines gave any clue as to what was unfolding in that terrible, shadowy place. Butch's yelps soon fell silent until all that remained was the coyote's gulping and slobbering as it feasted on the poor animal. Adios, Butch... He died doing what he loved, which I suppose is the best any of us can hope for. I turned my gaze back to the skunk, lying impassively in the middle of the street. A fat fly circled once, twice above it, before plopping lazily onto the mushed skull. As it settled down to eat, I turned my eyes away.

Jesus... what a lousy, godforsaken day this was. It seemed that Death was *everywhere*.

I walked on.

END

ALSO OUT ON FAR WEST

farwestpress.com

+1 (541) FAR-WEST